Time Pieces

for
B flat Saxophone

Music through the Ages in Two Volumes

Volume 2

Ian Denley

The Associated Board of
the Royal Schools of Music

CONTENTS

Time Pieces for B flat Saxophone

Volume 2

for Sharon

1692 ## Rondeau and Dance for the Haymakers

from *The Fairy Queen*

Henry Purcell
(1659–1695)

RONDEAU

Allegretto ♩ = *c*.100

Fine

AB 2769

D.C. al Fine

DANCE FOR THE HAYMAKERS

Allegro con spirito ♩ = 144–152

1729 Sinfonia
from Cantata No. 156, BWV 156

Johann Sebastian Bach
(1685–1750)

1773 Menuetto e Trio

from Symphony No. 25, K. 183

Wolfgang Amadeus Mozart
(1756–1791)

TRIO

Fine

Menuetto D.C. al Fine

1801 Allegro molto

from Serenade Op. 25

Ludwig van Beethoven
(1770–1827)

AB 2769

CODA

D.C. al Coda

1872 Orchestral solo

from *L'arlésienne*, Suite I

Georges Bizet
(1838–1875)

AB 2769

1888   **Two Little Pearls**

Antonín Dvořák
(1841–1904)

1. In a Ring!

D.C. al Fine

2. Grandpa Dances with Grandma

1900 Entry of the Gladiators

Op. 68

Julius Fučik
(1872–1916)

Time Pieces for B flat Saxophone

Volume 2

for Sharon

1692 ### Rondeau and Dance for the Haymakers

Henry Purcell
(1659–1695)

from *The Fairy Queen*

RONDEAU

Allegretto ♩ = *c*.100

Fine

D.C. al Fine

AB 2769

DANCE FOR THE HAYMAKERS

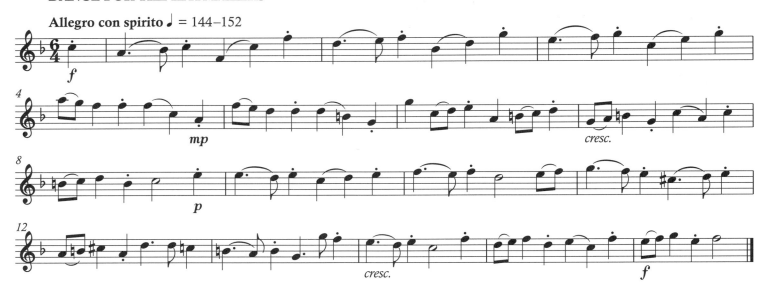

1729 Sinfonia
from Cantata No. 156, BWV 156

Johann Sebastian Bach
(1685–1750)

1773 Menuetto e Trio

from Symphony No. 25, K. 183

Wolfgang Amadeus Mozart
(1756–1791)

Menuetto D.C. al Fine

1801 Allegro molto

from Serenade Op. 25

Ludwig van Beethoven
(1770–1827)

1872 Orchestral solo

from *L'arlésienne*, Suite I

Georges Bizet
(1838–1875)

1888 Two Little Pearls

Antonín Dvořák
(1841–1904)

1. In a Ring!

2. Grandpa Dances with Grandma

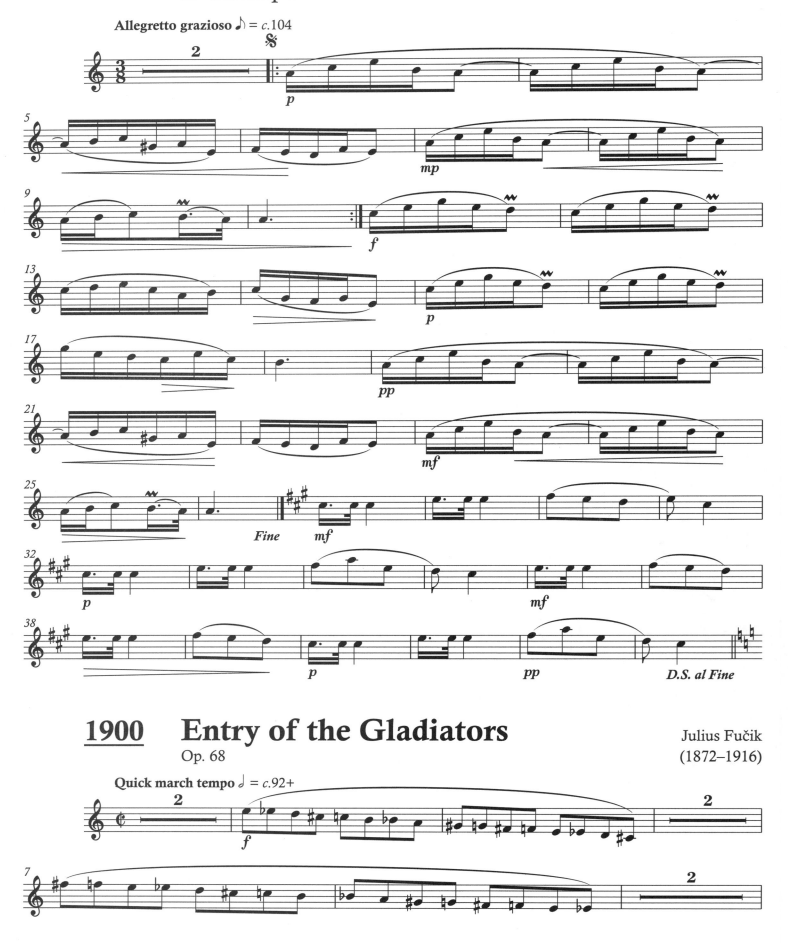

1900 **Entry of the Gladiators**
Op. 68

Julius Fučik
(1872–1916)

1905 Pavane pour une infante défunte

Maurice Ravel
(1875–1937)

AB 2769

1928 Tango-Ballade

from *The Threepenny Opera*

Kurt Weill
(1900–1950)

1945 Prelude No. 2
from *Six Preludes*, Op. 23

Lennox Berkeley
(1903–1989)

1945 Clockwork Doll
from *Six Children's Pieces*, Op. 69

Dmitry Shostakovich
(1906–1975)

1953 March

from *Three Youthful Pieces*

Witold Lutosławski
(1913–1994)

2000 New Age Tango

John McLeod
(b. 1934)

Printed in England by Caligraving Ltd, Thetford, Norfolk

Music origination by
Barnes Music Engraving Ltd, East Sussex

1905 Pavane pour une infante défunte

Maurice Ravel
(1875–1937)

* slow spread

1928 Tango-Ballade

from *The Threepenny Opera*

Kurt Weill
(1900–1950)

AB 2769

1945 Prelude No. 2

from *Six Preludes*, Op. 23

Lennox Berkeley
(1903–1989)

1945 Clockwork Doll

from *Six Children's Pieces*, Op. 69

Dmitry Shostakovich
(1906–1975)

1953 March

from *Three Youthful Pieces*

Witold Lutosławski
(1913–1994)

Allegro ♩ = 108–112

AB 2769

2000 New Age Tango

John McLeod
(b. 1934)

Tempo di Tango ♩ = *c*.60

Music origination by
Barnes Music Engraving Ltd, East Sussex
Printed in England by Caligraving Ltd, Thetford, Norfolk

AB 2769

8:08